D1243896

Penrod
The Dancing Emperor Penguin

by

Henrietta Roginski
author & illustrator

Hagaman, New York

MUSICAL SPHERES

HAVE fun REAding
SPENROd
Henrietta Reginski

One day in sunny but cold Antarctica, Penrod, a year-old emperor penguin, shed the last of his baby-chick feathers. He was dressed in a new black and white penguin suit that looked like a tuxedo.

Penrod said to his parents, "Look at me. I have a new suit!" Papa Penguin said, "How handsome and dignified you look. You are truly an emperor penguin!" Mama Penguin teasingly added, "Keep you new suit snowy-clean. Someday you will hear the mysterious Music of the Spheres, and you will go dancing in your tuxedo." Penrod wondered what the Music of the Spheres was, but he was too excited about his new suit to ask. * * * * *

   The penguin family was standing on an ice ledge not far
from home. Penrod looked at his reflection in the water below.
His tuxedo with its golden band around his neck and ears was
handsome, indeed!

It seemed only yesterday that Penrod had been a young chick with soft, gray feathers. He loved to stay in the middle of the crèche, a nestful of fluffy-feathered young penguins huddled together to keep warm. Somehow, at this crèche of courtesy, the penguins had all learned to take turns in sharing this prized center within the moving circle of warmth against the winds and snows of Antarctica. * * * * *

4

Now, out of the crèche and dressed in his new suit, Penrod wanted to learn more about himself and his surroundings, perhaps even finding the Music of the Spheres. Penrod already knew he could make penguin calls with the other young penguins — calls that sounded like WHIST . . . WHIST. "Is this music?" he wondered. Penrod decided to try his own solo.

Waddling to a quiet place between two slopes of ice and snow, he started his penguin call. Penrod smiled when he discovered his call bounced back from the slopes, like an echo echoing WHIST . . . WHIST. Pleased with this duet, Penrod shouted, "My echo and I are making music!" * * * * *

Using a glistening icicle as a sword, Penrod knighted his friend Sir Echo Echo, just like in the stories of chivalry that Papa Penguin read to him. Penrod had fun playing this game of knighthood and asked Sir Echo Echo to help him in his quest to find the Music of the Spheres.

That evening, the sky was clear, and Papa Penguin decided to give Penrod his first astronomy lesson. He began by teaching Penrod about the stars — especially the vast path of dancing lights called the Milky Way.

Papa Penguin then pointed out the <u>Aurora Australis</u>, the beautiful green and pink ribbons of light radiating across the southern sky.

Papa Penguin next talked about the planets and the musical sounds they made throughout the universe. "But when can I hear this music?" Penrod asked. Papa Penguin answered, "You will not hear the music tonight, Penrod. The Music of the Spheres is like magic and happens only at special times when the air and water currents are just right. Besides, it is already past your bedtime!"

The next day, Penrod discovered some krill and squid, which the water currents had just splashed ashore. He shared his delicious feast with the other hungry young penguins, and ate the treats with much delight, dribbling on his penguin suit.

After Penrod slowly waddled home, Mama Penguin pointed to a small, snowy hill in the distance, saying, "Toboggan on your tummy to clean your suit." It took Penrod at least seven toboggan rides to make his suit clean. * * * * *

He made his way home again over the snowy ice floe, slipping and flipping like a pinwheel into the water with a big splash. * * * * *

Penrod discovered he did not sink. Using his feet as rudders and his flippers as paddles, he splashed and swam with the other young penguins.

Penrod soon leaped ashore to play with Sir Echo Echo again. He waddled to his quiet place between the two icy, snowy slopes and sang his WHIST . . . WHIST duet with Sir Echo Echo. After many encores, Penrod suddenly stopped and stared. Air and water currents were swirling around the ice floe in a most unusual fashion. * * * * *

He listened intently. Yes, he was hearing harps and cellos. But, of course! It was the Music of the Spheres! For Penrod, it was serendipity — his biggest discovery yet! "So this is what Mama and Papa meant by the Music of the Spheres," he mused. Yes! He wanted to dance in his tuxedo, just as Mama Penguin had said he would.

Penrod's black webbed feet waddled awkwardly at first. Then, more gracefully, he danced in a circle. His WHIST . . . WHIST calls and those of Sir Echo Echo harmonized with the swirling Music of the Spheres.

Penrod picked up an icicle and waved it around. Like magic, it became a glistening conductor's baton!

Lo and behold! A parade of all the young penguins followed Penrod as he waved his baton and danced in bigger circles. Even the parent penguins joined in the widening circle, which now reached the outer edge of the ice floe.

Penrod, revelling in the magic of the Music of the Spheres, led the parade, dancing off the ice floe with his big splash — a solo, of course! All the dancing emperor penguins followed him for a swim in the ice-cooling waters of Antarctica.

GLOSSARY

Antarctica: A continent composed of the Polar Regions at the South Pole.

Astronomy: The study of stars, planets and other heavenly spheres.

Aurora Australis: Southern lights of the Southern Hemisphere which move as luminous lights with the southern winds (similar to the Aurora Borealis, northern lights of the Northern Hemisphere).

Chivalry: Age of knighthood, characterized by honor, courtesy and gallantry.

Crèche: A nestling place for baby chick penguins where they huddle together to keep warm.

Emperor Penguin: (Species Aptenodytes forsteri) A flightless bird, largest of the penguin family, living solely in Antarctica, weighing approximately 90 pounds, standing approximately 4 feet tall, people-friendly (U. S. Air National Guard personnel fly supplies to the National Science Foundation researchers in Antarctica).

Ice floe: A large floating mass of sea ice and snow.

Krill: Shrimp-like food eaten by penguins.

Milky Way: A galaxy or large grouping of millions of stars merging into a brilliant path of starry light across the sky.

Music of the Spheres: An idea proposed by Pythagoras, an ancient Greek philosopher and mathematician. He theorized that, since the planets move in their orbits at different rates of motion, they create a vibration that produces a musical harmony in tune with all the other celestial spheres of the universe.

Quest: A hunt or search of adventure and discovery as undertaken by knights of medieval times in pursuit of something heroic.

Serendipity: A surprise in unexpectedly finding something delightful.

Squid: A small, long-tapered fish eaten by penguins.

Tuxedo: Black, semi-formal evening clothes worn by men.

Waddle: To walk with short steps, and to sway from side to side.

ANTARCTICA